NO LONGER PROPERTY OF
ANYTHINK LIBRARIES/
RANGEVIEW LIBRARY DISTRICT

D0468534

Does FRANKENSTEIN Get Hungry?

JOHN SOLIMINE

G. P. Putnam's Sons

Sometimes in the dead of night
when I find myself awake,
my mind will start to wander places
that make my stomach ache.

As I sit here in the gloom,
things begin to crawl and creep—
so I ask myself these questions
to help me fall asleep.

Does **FRANKENSTEIN** get hungry?
Would he like a bowl of soup?
Bet he'd like the Oatmeal Munchies
I sell for my Camp Scout troop!

Does a **ZOMBIE** go to school?
I think I have a hunch:
Her mother packs her goopy brains
and a juicy box for lunch!

Are **MUMMIES** fond of long bike rides
just like normal folks?
Or do their crusty bandages
get tangled in the spokes?

Do **GHOSTS** have pets like dogs and cats,
maybe a hamster they named Fred?
Do they teach them silly tricks
like roll over and play dead?

Does **Dracula** have to floss his fangs
to clean off sticky plaque
when he eats blood sausages
with pickles as a snack?

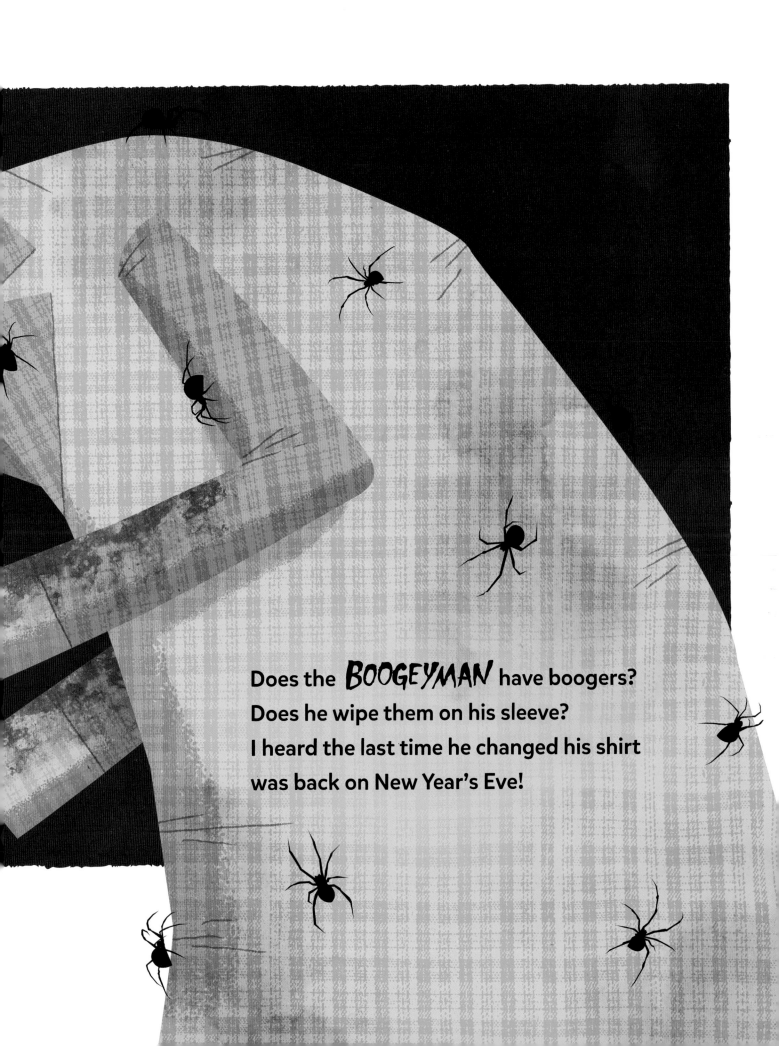

Does the *BOOGEYMAN* have boogers?
Does he wipe them on his sleeve?
I heard the last time he changed his shirt
was back on New Year's Eve!

Do warty WITCHES with black-striped britches
have to clean their rooms?
There's no excuse for being messy
when you ride around on brooms!

Do CREEPY CLOWNS with basset hounds
ever get the blues?
I know one thing to cheer them up:
a chorus of kazoos!

Do **GIANT LIZARDS** have little sisters
who break their favorite toys?
And when it's time to go to sleep,
it's NOISE! NOISE! NOISE!

Do **WEREWOLVES** have cold noses
like all the neighborhood mutts?
After howling at the moon,
do they sniff each other's butts?

Does the **THING** that lives beneath my bed
get lonely under there?
Its only friend is a musty, dusty,
one-eyed teddy bear.

All these questions make the ghoulish appear foolish
and the ghostly mostly meek.
Being scared is so silly now that
monsters seem so weak!

I guess my list is finished—
it's nearly half past three!
Last question for all monsters:
Aren't YOU the ones
who should be scared of ME?

FOR JENNY AND LOU

**Special thanks to Jenny for
her color and storytelling expertise**

G. P. PUTNAM'S SONS
an imprint of Penguin Random House LLC
375 Hudson Street
New York, NY 10014

Copyright © 2018 by John Solimine.
Penguin supports copyright. Copyright fuels creativity, encourages diverse voices, promotes free speech, and creates
a vibrant culture. Thank you for buying an authorized edition of this book and for complying with copyright laws by not
reproducing, scanning, or distributing any part of it in any form without permission. You are supporting writers
and allowing Penguin to continue to publish books for every reader.

G. P. Putnam's Sons is a registered trademark of Penguin Random House LLC.

Library of Congress Cataloging-in-Publication Data
Names: Solimine, John, author.
Title: Does Frankenstein get hungry? / John Solimine.
Description: New York, NY : G. P. Putnam's Sons, [2018]
Summary: A young girl banishes her fear of monsters by imagining a series of
questions and answers that make the ghoulish seem foolish.
Identifiers: LCCN 2017040087 | ISBN 9780399546419 (hardcover : alk. paper) |
ISBN 9780399546501 (ebook) | ISBN 9780399546426 (ebook)
Subjects: | CYAC: Stories in rhyme. | Monsters—Fiction. | Questions and answers—Fiction. | Fear of the dark—Fiction.
Classification: LCC PZ8.3.S6953 Doe 2018 | DDC [E]—dc23
LC record available at https://lccn.loc.gov/2017040087

Manufactured in China by RR Donnelley Asia Printing Solutions Ltd.
ISBN 9780399546419
1 3 5 7 9 10 8 6 4 2

Design by Eileen Savage. Text set in Mikado.
The art for this book was created with pencil, pen, and Photoshop.
Additional artwork on pages 4-5 and 28-29 by Jack Bonasso, Zane Ewers, and Lou Solimine.